Little DRAGON and the New Baby

First Edition

Sky Pony Press books may be purchased in bulk at special discounts for sales promotion, corporate gifts, fund-raising, or educational purposes. Special editions can also be created to specifications. For details, contact the Special Sales Department, Sky Pony Press, 307 West 36th Street, 11th Floor, New York, NY 10018 or info@skyhorsepublishing.com.

Sky Pony® is a registered trademark of Skyhorse Publishing, Inc.®, a Delaware corporation.
Visit our website at www.skyponypress.com.

10 9 8 7 6 5 4 3 2 1

Manufactured in China, November 2017
This product conforms to CPSIA 2008

Library of Congress Cataloging-in-Publication Data is available on file.

Cover design by Kate Gartner
Cover illustration by Deborah Cuneo

Print ISBN: 978-1-5107-1268-3
Ebook ISBN: 978-1-5107-1269-0

Little DRAGON and the New Baby

Story and pictures by **Deborah Cuneo**

Sky Pony Press
New York

Mom and Dad had a big surprise for Little Dragon!
Surprise? Little dragons love surprises . . .

. . . sometimes.

My RO
MOM
ME

Maybe having a new brother or sister wouldn't be so bad.

But Little Dragon
wasn't so sure about
sharing his room.

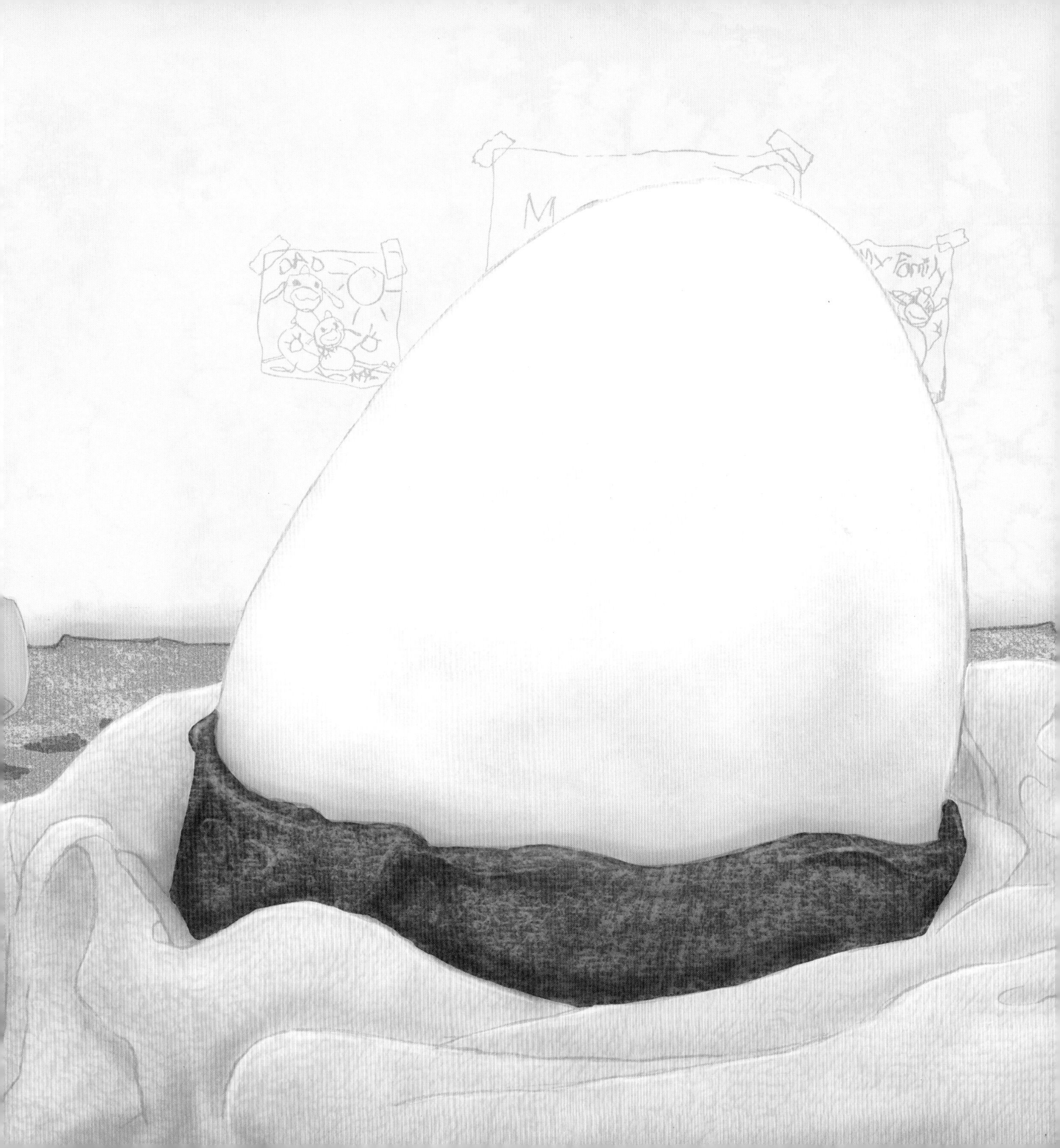
DAD
my Family

He was definitely not in the mood for company right now.

Little Dragon felt like nothing could make this better!

Then, he had a great idea!

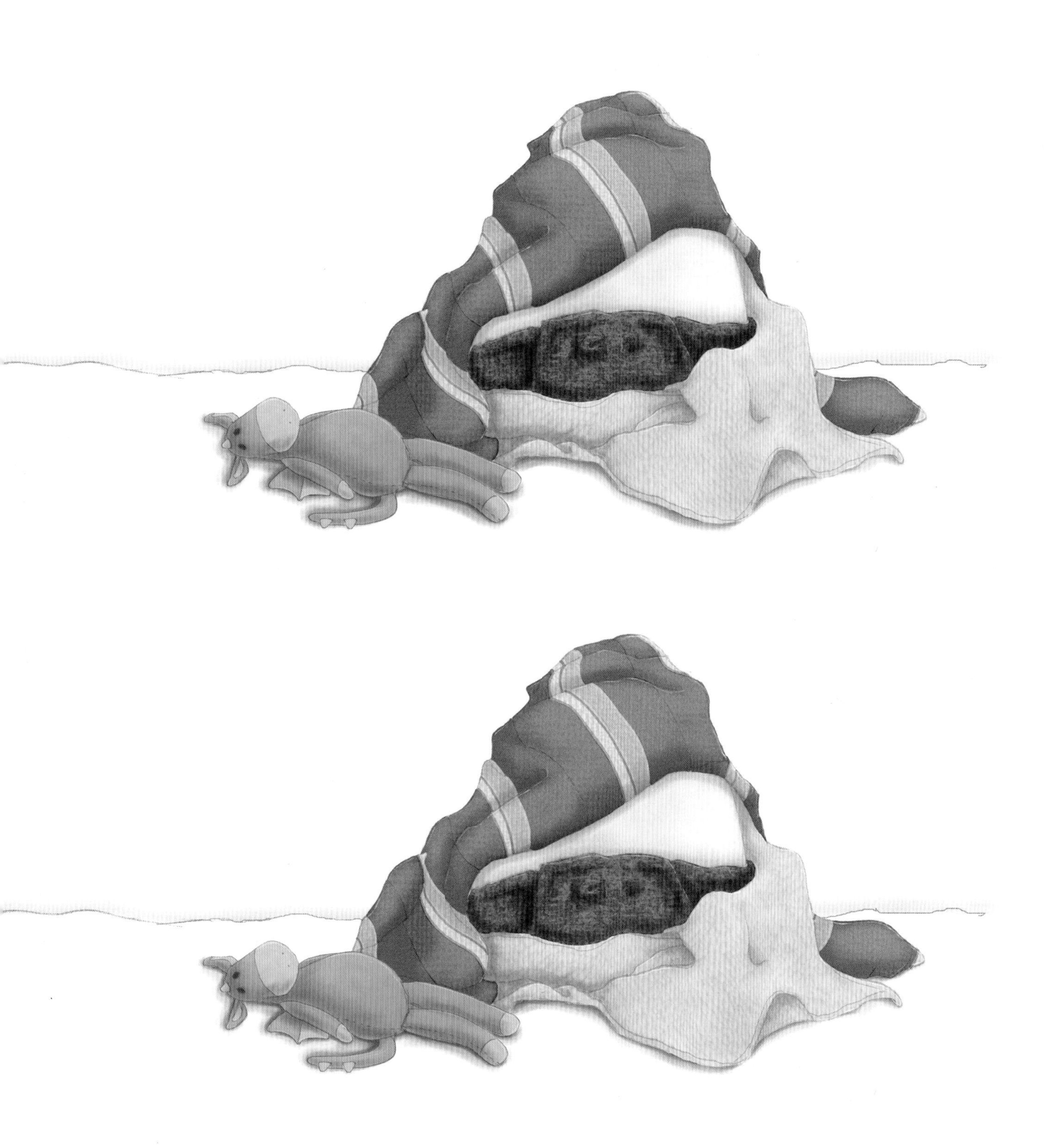

Mom didn't think his idea was all that great, though.

She was right.

CRAA

Something was happening!
Was it his fault?

He hoped no one would notice . . .

My ROOM

. . . but they did!

TWO?

They *were* kind of cute.

Maybe things would be OK after all.

Maybe . . .